To my mom and my husband—
for each providing a home full of soothing sounds
—Mickie Matheis

To Uncle Billy and Uncle Casper
—Bonnie Leick

Text copyright © 2012 by Mickie Matheis
Illustrations copyright © 2012 by Bonnie Leick

randomhouse.com/kids

Educators and librarians, for a variety of teaching tools, visit us at randomhouse.com/teachers

Library of Congress Cataloging-in-Publication Data
Matheis, Mickie.
Bedtime for Boo / by Mickie Matheis ; illustrated by Bonnie Leick.
p. cm.
Summary: Boo, the youngest ghost in his family, is excited on his first night of haunting but soon tires and,
upon returning home, falls asleep to the familiar groaning, creaking, and rattling of his house.
ISBN 978-0-375-86991-4 (trade) — ISBN 978-0-375-96991-1 (lib. bdg.)
[1. Ghosts—Fiction. 2. Noise—Fiction. 3. Bedtime—Fiction.] I. Title.
PZ7.M42425Re 2012
[E]—dc23
2011018058

PRINTED IN CHINA
10 9 8 7 6 5 4 3 2 1

Bedtime for BOO

By Mickie Matheis

Illustrated by Bonnie Leick

 A GOLDEN BOOK • NEW YORK

In a big dark house
Sitting high on a hill . . .

With a rusty front gate
And cracked glass windows,
Overgrown with weeds
And crawling with shadows,
There lived a family of ghosts.

The littlest one was Boo.

The ghosts were in high spirits—
A-haunting they were going!
Now for the first time,
Boo would go, too.
He couldn't wait to stay up late—
Just like big ghosts do!

Boo flew through the night sky,
Laughing out loud,
To play hide-and-seek
in the silver-streaked clouds.

He waved at the stars
And winked at the moon
And whistled a happy-*ghost*-lucky tune.

The wind swirled the leaves,
Swept them up from the ground,
And Boo jumped aboard
the merry-*ghost*-round.

Then Boo spooked an owl—
It flew off with a *WHOOOO!*
And just as he wondered what else to do,
The fun of the ghosts' night out was through.

Time for bed, sleepyhead,
Mama Ghost said back at home.
How can I sleep
    when I'm . . . not . . . tired?
Boo yawned.

I'll tell you how, Boo, Mama cooed.
Listen to the sounds of the house.

Just close your eyes and hush—
Can you hear the ghosts float by
with a *WHOOSH*?
WHOOSH, WHOOSH

I hear them! said Boo. Do you?
Yes, said Mama. *Now lie down.*
Let's use our ears.
Tell me, little Boo,
        what else can you hear?

I hear some bats
flapping—
FLAPPING,
FLAPPING
And footsteps
tapping—
TAPPING,
TAPPING

There are spiders

clicking—

CLICKING,
CLICKING

And an old clock

ticking—

TICKING,
TICKING

As ghosts float by

with a *WHOOSH*.

Those sound so nice, Mama sighed.
And there are mice! Boo said.

Scurrying around squeaking—
SQUEAKING, SQUEAKING
As doors are creaking—
CREAKING, CREAKING

There are witches cackling—
CACKLING, CACKLING
And skeletons rattling—
RATTLING, RATTLING
As ghosts float by
with a *WHOOSH*.

There's more, Mama said.
The floors! Boo answered.

They're groaning—
GROANING, GROANING
Under monsters moaning—
MORNING, MORNING

I hear wolves howling—
HOWLING, HOWLING
And something growling—
GROWLING, GROWLING
As ghosts float by
with a *WHOOSH*.

Very good, Boo, murmured Mama.
What's still missing?

Black cats hissing—
HISSING, HISSING
And the wind whistling—
WHISTLING, WHISTLING

Then Boo grew still. So Mama whispered:

While thunder is rumbling—
RUMBLING, RUMBLING
And the rain comes drumming—
DRUMMING, DRUMMING
As ghosts float by
*with a **WHOOSH**.*

The room was very quiet.
After a while, Mama Ghost opened
 her eyes for a peek . . .
And sure enough,
Little Boo was finally fast asleep.

Good night, Boo.